Usborne English R

Level 1

Sleeping Beauty

Retold by Mairi Mackinnon

Illustrated by Elena Selivanova

English language consultant: Peter Viney

Contents

You can listen to the story online here:
www.usborneenglishreaders.com/
sleepingbeauty

Long ago, a king and queen lived in a castle in the forest. The king loved the queen, and the queen loved the king, but for a long time they had no children. The queen wanted a child more than anything else.

One day, she told her husband, "I'm going to have a baby."

"That's wonderful!" the king said.
"I'm so happy."

When the queen's baby was born,
there was a party. Servants cleaned the
castle from top to bottom, and the cooks
worked night and day in the kitchens.

The king and queen asked all their
friends to come to the party. They asked
seven fairies to be the baby's godmothers.

The castle was full of light and music. The queen held her baby girl, and the baby smiled. The king stood up. "Dear friends," he said. "This is our daughter. Her name is Rose."

All the party guests had presents for the little princess. The fairies had their own very special presents.

"Your daughter is going to be beautiful," said one fairy.

"She's going to be kind, too," said another.

"And clever," said another.

"And good at dancing," said another.

"And good at singing…"

"She's going to have lots of friends…"

"STOP!" said a loud voice. A fairy in a long, black dress stood at the other end of the castle hall. "What is this party? Why didn't you invite ME?"

"We didn't know…" said the queen.

"We didn't think…" said the king.

"Well, think about this," said the fairy. "I have a present for your daughter, too. When she is sixteen years old, she's going to hurt her little hand on a spindle, and then she's going to die!"

"You can't do that!" said the queen –
but the fairy turned and left the room,
with a terrible laugh.

"Don't cry," said another voice. It was
the seventh fairy. "I didn't have time to
give the princess my present. I can't stop
bad magic, but I can make it better.

Rose isn't going to die. She's only going
to fall asleep for a hundred years. I know
it's a long time, but it's better than dying."

The next day, the king sent his servants across the country. Now nobody could use spindles for spinning. Everyone had to bring their spindles out and burn them.

The king saw the light from a hundred fires. "Now Rose is safe," he said.

Rose grew into a beautiful, kind girl, just as the fairies said. Her parents loved her very much. Sometimes they worried about her, but the king told the queen, "There are no spindles in the country. Nothing bad can happen."

When Rose was sixteen, there was another wonderful party at the castle. There was music and dancing, and all Rose's friends were there.

Late in the evening, the princess had an idea. "Let's play a game," she said. "I'm going to hide, and you must come and find me. I'm *very* good at hiding." She laughed and ran out of the hall.

"I need to find a good hiding place," she thought. She saw some narrow stairs, and a little door at the top. She went up the stairs, opened the door and saw an old woman in a chair by the window.

The old woman had lots of white wool. She was making the wool into thread with a strange wooden thing. Rose watched her. "What are you doing?" she asked. "What is that?"

"I'm spinning, my dear," said the old woman. "This is a spindle. Would you like to try?"

Rose picked up the wool, and tried not to break the thread. She took the spindle, turned it quickly around and then caught it. "Oh!"

"Is something wrong, my dear?"

"I hurt my hand. It doesn't matter, I…" Rose never finished the sentence. She fell asleep on the hard stone floor.

In the middle of the party, the music stopped. Suddenly, everyone was very tired. "Something's wrong," said the queen. "Where's Rose?"

They looked everywhere, and soon found the narrow stairs. In the room at the top they found the sleeping princess and a frightened old woman. They tried to wake Rose, but they couldn't.

"Take her to her bedroom," said the king. Carefully, the servants carried the princess to her bed.

"Oh, my dear beautiful daughter," said the queen sadly. She and the king left the room.

Everywhere in the castle, people started to fall asleep. The party guests slept with their heads on the dinner tables. The servants sat down at the side of the room and closed their eyes. The cooks in the kitchens put down their knives, sat by the fire and slept. Even the horses and the dogs and the birds fell asleep.

"What's happening? What can we do?" the queen asked the king.

"You need to sleep, too," said a gentle voice. It was the seventh fairy. She took them back to their places in the hall. The king held the queen's hand, and soon they were both asleep. The fairy left the hall.

She stopped outside the castle walls
and put her hand gently to the ground.
Wild roses grew up and hid the walls, the
windows and even the roof. The forest
grew up around the roses. Soon nobody
remembered the king, the queen or
Princess Rose.

A hundred years later, a prince was riding in the forest when he saw something between the trees. He rode nearer.

"Wild roses!" he said. "They're growing over something…"

He jumped down from his horse, and started cutting the roses with his sword.

Soon he could see a way through the roses to the castle.

First he found the sleeping dogs and horses. "This is some strong magic," he thought. He went inside and found the cooks asleep in the kitchen, and the servants and guests in the hall. "They're not dead," he said, "but how can I wake them?"

He walked through the castle, and in every room he found more people asleep.

In the last room, he found Princess Rose. "She's so beautiful," he said. "Surely she's the most beautiful girl in the world." He held her hand, and the princess opened her eyes and smiled.

Everywhere in the castle, people started waking. The cooks woke up on the cold kitchen floor. The servants jumped up and started to work. The guests in the hall were very surprised when they woke beside tables of cold food.

Princess Rose was laughing at the prince. "Your clothes are so strange!"

"*My* clothes?" said the prince. "My grandmother's grandmother wore a dress like yours! It's a lovely dress," he said quickly.

"Come downstairs," said Rose. "Everyone is waking up. I can hear them."

When Rose and the prince walked into the hall, the king and queen opened their eyes. "Rose!" said the queen. She held out her arms to her daughter.

"And who is this young man?" asked the king with a smile.

Suddenly the seventh fairy was there. "This young man is a prince," she said. "He and Rose would like to get married – and they are going to be very happy together, I know."

About the story

Charles Perrault lived in France from 1628-1703. For most of his life, he worked for the French government, but he was always very interested in books and stories too. In 1695, Perrault lost his government job and started writing stories for his children. *Sleeping Beauty* is one of these stories. Perrault took the idea from a much older story. He added the part about the princess and everyone in the castle sleeping for a hundred years.

Perrault's stories were soon very popular, not only in France but all over Europe. Today, people know and love these stories all around the world. This kind of story is called a fairy story. Fairy stories are often about kings, queens, princes and princesses, fairies and magic. Some other fairy stories by Perrault are *Little Red Riding Hood*, *Cinderella* and *Puss in Boots*.

Activities

The answers are on page 32.

What is Rose thinking?

Choose the right sentence for each picture.

A.
"His clothes are so strange!"

B.
"We'd like to get married."

C.
"My hand hurts."

D.
"What a wonderful party!"

What happened when?

Can you put these pictures in the right order?

A.

The princess opened her eyes and smiled.

B.

He started cutting the roses with his sword.

C.

"This is our daughter. Her name is Rose."

D.

They tried to wake Rose, but they couldn't.

E.

"I have a present for your daughter, too."

F.

She saw an old woman in a chair by the window

Castle life

Choose the right word to finish each sentence.

safe   long   beautiful   dead

wonderful   short   careful   late

1.

"That's ....," said the king.

2.

"I know it's a .... time, but it's better than dying."

3.

Rose grew into a ...., kind girl.

4.

"They're not ...., but how can I wake them?"

A fairy tale

One word in each sentence is wrong.
Can you choose the right word instead?

1.

"Your daughter is going to be real," said one fairy.

beautiful   true   perfect

2.

"I can't stop bad magic, but I can make it easier."

safer   slower   better

3.

Lovely roses grew up and hid the walls.

Friendly   Wild   Useful

4.

"They are going to be very sleepy together, I know."

happy   special   funny

What happened next?

Choose the right sentence for each picture.

1. **The king saw the light from a hundred fires.**

   A. "Now nobody can learn to spin," he said.

   B. "Now Rose is safe," he said.

2. **"What are you doing?" Rose asked.**

   A. "I'm spinning, my dear," said the old woman.

   B. "I'm trying to hurt you," said the old woman.

3. **Everywhere, people started waking.**

   A. The servants jumped up and ran away.

   B. The servants jumped up and started to work.

Word list

castle (n) a large old building with strong stone walls.

cook (n) someone who works in a kitchen and makes meals.

dear (adj) you say 'dear' to someone you like very much or love.

fall asleep, fell asleep (v) to start to sleep.

gentle (adj) careful and kind.

godmother (n) a woman who is usually not in your family, but who promises to help you when you are growing up.

grow, grew (v) to become older (for a person), or to become bigger (for a plant).

guest (n) when you have a party, the people that come to your party are your guests.

hall (n) a very large room in a castle, or the first room in a house.

hide (v) when you hide, no one can see you or find you.

hurt (v) when something hurts you, you feel pain in a part of your body.

kind (adj) good and nice to other people.

narrow (adj) thin, not wide. If a room
is narrow, the walls are very close.

rose (n) a kind of flower. People often grow roses
in gardens. 'Rose' can also be a girl's name.

servant (n) someome who works for
another person, especially in their home.

spin (v) to make **thread** (n). Thread
makes cloth, and cloth makes clothes.

spindle (n) in the past, people used spindles
to make thread, especially from wool.

sword (n) in the past, soldiers used
swords for fighting. Swords were made
of metal, and were very sharp.

wild (adj) something that grows naturally,
not in a garden or on a farm.

wonderful (adj) really good and special.

wooden (adj) made of wood.

wool (n) a sheep has wool. Sheep's
wool is used to make clothes.

Answers

What is Rose thinking?
1. D
2. C
3. A
4. B

What happened when?
C, E, F, D, B, A.

Castle life
1. wonderful
2. long
3. beautiful
4. dead

A fairy tale
1. ~~real~~ beautiful
2. ~~easier~~ better
3. ~~Lovely~~ Wild
4. ~~sleepy~~ happy

What happened next?
1. B
2. A
3. B

You can find information about other Usborne English Readers here:
www.usborneenglishreaders.com

Designed by Hope Reynolds

Series designer: Laura Nelson Norris

Edited by Jane Chisholm

With thanks to Andy Prentice

Digital imaging: Nick Wakeford

Page 24: picture of Charles Perrault © White Images/Scala, Florence.

First published in 2018 by Usborne Publishing Ltd.,
Usborne House, 83-85 Saffron Hill, London EC1N 8RT, England.
www.usborne.com Copyright © 2018 Usborne Publishing Ltd.